FIRST CLASS FIRST TIME

Short Stories of
First Time
Erotic Encounters

RICHARD T. GRAYSON

Copyright © 2021 Richard T. Grayson

All rights reserved.

ISBN: 9798669646486

TICKET TO RIDE 7
CHERRY BLOSSOM 41
RED HEAT 71

TICKET TO RIDE

Virgin Trains

I am on my way to London on a Virgin train to fly back home to Frankfurt for the weekend. My first-class coach is deserted and the rest of the train seems abandoned as well at this late hour.

Today's workshop with my client was a grand success. My excellent performance should secure the next phases of the project, worth millions. This also means I will continue to work in the UK for quite a while longer. My consulting engagement with this client already lasts 6 months and I enjoy the travels a lot. This is my first assignment abroad, and I want to explore much more of the liberties one has far from home.

After the workshop, I had taken my client out for a quick feedback pint. Now it's past 9 o'clock and I am already slightly inebriated. I made myself comfortable in the last coach of the train, hoping to have it all to myself for the 90 minutes ride into Paddington. Entertaining a room packed with client senior management for a full day has exhausted my social skills. All I want is to enjoy my peace; and another lager or two from the board service.

One advantage of being a ridiculously expensive IT security expert is that you travel first-class. However, as Vesper Lynd put it in Casino Royal, 'there are Dinner Jackets and there are Dinner Jackets'. The first-class on this Virgin train connection is quite rundown. The out-of-control air condition heats the compartments to a smelly thirty degrees Celsius. Water drips from the ceiling in the passageway between coaches even on dry days; likely the same water not available in the sinks and flushes of the toilets. These are in an unacceptable condition altogether. And the worn upholstery of the armchairs looks like living inside them might be several still unspecified life forms yet to be discovered.

Unfortunately, the sixties interior design lacks the morbid charm of the fading Empire that makes so many other shortcomings of contemporary England bearable. Since it's not style and comfort, what justifies the outrageous price of this questionable first-class pleasure? And how on earth did Virgin preserve its reputation of being particularly customer-friendly? It isn't the catering service included in the ticket price. The food is mediocre at best. One has to make up for it with the inexhaustible supply of drinks they provide.

Virgin Trains excellent reputation might best be explained with the forbearance the natives had to develop to consistently renounce the end of British world domination and recognize signs of greatness beyond the fantastic imperial architecture of London. Englishmen find German efficiency silly. They don't hate us for it, like the French do, but they joke about us. And then again, they hire people like me to help them make things more efficient.

May be, though, the British have a point, I contemplate, as the train stops again on open tracks a few miles from the next station. In the recent months of me traveling back and forth between London and my client's country side location, several times children have been playing on the tracks, causing the train to stop in the middle of nowhere. Since the rail network is in an even more miserable condition than the compartment cars, British trains travel at a very moderate speed. It may well be that these young lives owe their continued existence only to the most illustrative privatization flop in history. There might be a higher plan to all of this, I conclude, while I finish my third lager.

As we eventually make it to the station, a young lad enters the carriage. He is the cliché British working-class chap with a wide tooth gap and a gaze that is just as cockeyed as it is cocky and confrontational. Even though it's just above freezing levels outside, he wears only a red hooded Everlast sweater and even short white jeans. Curly red-blond hair sticks out from the base cap hidden underneath his hood.

The lad gawks down the aisle, drops first his backpack and then himself into the plushy seats two rows from where I sit.

Only people who enjoy being looked at wear white jeans these days. The short pants lay bare a first excellent reason for a healthy confidence level, though: remarkably brawny sprinters legs with slender ankles plugged into high chucks worn with neither laces nor socks. The proprietor of these impressive legs might be in his early twenties and, from the looks of it, quite possibly a first-class athlete, but not a first-class passenger.

Virgin Trains does not call it second class, like the

Deutsche Bahn does, but standard class. I like this non-discriminatory term much better. Nobody wants to be second class. To be standard, and thus average, is no problem; at least for a good German. Standard may even mean *the* standard, a quasi-official seal of quality, as it were. The possibilities of positive interpretation are manifold.

The British, however, seem to be an aspiring nation, because the first-class usually has more coaches than the standard class. Then again: most of these coaches are always orphaned.

While pondering the class issues in modern British society, the right side of my brain demands more attention for my unknown traveling companion and his way above standard physique.

I get up from my window seat, fetch my notebook from the hat rack, sit back down, this time in the aisle seat and place my notebook in a position that allows me to direct my view towards the thighs and calves on display yet pretend to be looking at my screen.

As the lad slides down his seat, the trousers get pulled up higher and higher, revealing more and more of the impressive tear shaped quad muscles towering above his knees. The young man stares out of the window and occasionally monitors the aisle with an apathetic expression.

The air con defect turns into a desired feature because within minutes the heat convinces the young man to take off his hoody. He almost pulls off his shirt, too, when he wrestles the hoody over his head, briefly revealing two rows of cobblestones.

The skin tight black tank top is cut out to the solar plexus anyway, but as the lad pulls it back down the plunging neckline stops just short of revealing the belly button. A clunky Cuban link chain meanders along the hillsides of steep pec piles into the deep crevice with a driblet creek of sweat running down this cleavage. The young athlete's nipples are oddly positioned, much more centered than usual, looking like molehills on the highest peaks of the muscle mounts.

As he eventually lets go of the shirt and it bounces back, the collar seam gets stuck at the pointy nipples, leaving them exposed.

The young Adonis tosses his hoody and cap on top of his bag and reclines his chair. He stares out of the window; the collar seam finally springs back into shape; and my mind zooms out its focus from his hypnotizing teats.

Red, consciously disorganized curls falling over his eyes run only on the top of his head; sides and back are trimmed to millimeters. This is brave given his distinctive jug ears, even emphasized with large flesh tunnel plugs.

The lad pulls out his phone, puts in ear pods and seems to scroll through a playlist. He scans the train again before he closes his eyes to sink himself into the music.

After a while, the chunky chest starts bouncing to a silent rhythm. The twitching contractions look like a heart beating on the outside. I am so mesmerized by this pec dance that the lad catches me off guard when he suddenly opens his eyes and gazes straight at me. Instantly, I focus my sight on my notebook screen, anxious to look up to find out if he caught me staring.

From the corner of my eye, I see him turn to the window. I glance over carefully and try to convince myself the smirk on his face is a sign of him enjoying a great song.

With the smile, two pit marks emerge on his cheeks. A fizzy red mustache adorns his upper lip and a similarly fizzy goatee ornaments the tip of his longish chin. Padded lips and small soft eyes rimmed by long lashes frame a meaty British snub nose. Besides the grim gaze, his appearance is quite mellow.
The more I examine the details the more I develop a patronizing appreciation for what I interpret as a schoolyard bully that puts up a protective shield of ostentatious, in your face cockiness to hide his soft spots.

It's a trick of the trade I learned in a sales seminar a few years back: it is very hard, if not impossible, for people to hate you, when you truly like them. It is human nature. If sympathy is genuine, people have to like you back. When I meet people for the first time, I look for character traits I can develop affection for. Even before I know enough about them to identify those traits, I make up likable preliminary profile stories. This young athlete, until better insights are available, was a fat kid in school that got bullied a lot and when he got strong enough to be physically uncontestable, he protected his emotional vulnerability with a facade of ill-temperedness.

Then again, if the impressive athlete and I should get to talk, I would hope my adoration for his beautiful physique may send enough positive vibes to make him like me back. While I try to put together a script on how to establish such communication with the young chap eventually, he scans the trolley alley again. This time I'm much better prepared, instantly putting on a hard-thinking face while staring at my slide deck.

The fat-kid-turned-bully returns to playlist contemplation, only to reach for his base cap moments later. He adjusts the cap and the curls diligently for quite a while. It seems like an excuse to flex his mango-shaped biceps. While he makes them jump up and down, dancing to the silent tune, he absently gazes at hundreds of chimneys rushing by, allowing me to watch his show.

To count chimneys in the dark seems to have the same effect as counting sheep, so the lad leans back and closes his eyes again. Fortunate for me the music must have gone into crescendo just now because only seconds later the sleeping beauty revives once more, starting to accompany the silent sound by drumming with imaginary sticks. With every beat, every twist and turn of his wrists, his biceps twitch and his pecs bounce in tune.

It is well possible he knows that I'm watching, yet

whenever he looks up to check for danger ahead, I am quick to stare at my notebook. The game goes on for quite a while, until, on one of his inspections, he seems to spot something very unpleasant. Sudden panic fills his face. He turns around, seeking an escape route, only to be reminded that the train ends right behind him. He chews on the knuckle of his pointing finger, puts his feet up on the opposite chair, presses himself in his seat and seems to consider his options.

I turn around and see the ticket inspector opening the coach door. I don't know what his original plan was to start with. To hide in the men's room? To jump off at the next station whenever a ticket inspector approaches?

Whatever the plan was: it failed. This promises to get interesting.

"Tickets please", yells the approaching authority upon entering. He is not much taller than 5 feet and just as wide, squeezing his obese carcass through the narrow aisle.

I produce my ticket and hand it to him. His tiny hands barely reach out from the way too long sleeves of his uniform.

Next, he turns to my young friend: "Tickets!" The tone in his voice shows he is expecting trouble.

"Tickets!" he repeats twice as loud, to make sure the lad can hear him, since he is still wearing his ear pods.

"Oy yav lost me student ticket", the callow lad responds, continuing to gaze in the night.

"Can I see some ID then please?" the inspector requests languidly, like he is doing it for the hundredth time today.

FIRST CLASS FIRST TIME

"Oy dent bren anny."[1]

"I am afraid, Sir, in this case you will have to buy an extra ticket," says the inspector, now in the lecturing version of his squeaky voice.

The kid barks like a street dog that got cornered: "Oy told yaouw I yav a student ticket, don't Oy?"[2] he snaps, now facing the inspector, pulling out his ear pods.

"Well, you told me you do not have a ticket in your possession, didn't you? You have to be able to present the ticket upon inspection," recites the uniformed authority from the terms and conditions fine print, obviously enjoying the situation.
"And take your shoes off the seat, punk!" he orders in as deep a pitch as he can.

"Who am ya callen a poonk?"[3] grunts the suspected fare dodger with the intimidating tone a truly deep voice can produce, welcoming the opportunity to divert from the subject.

The triumph has disappeared from the intonation of the inspector when he mechanically chants: "You can either buy a ticket from me now or have your personal details collected by the police at the next stop. You will have two weeks to present a valid ticket for today at one of our customer service centers."

"Oy told yaouw me ticket got stolen. An' so was me wodja. Stop mither me. Go and play up your own end!"[4]

---

[1] I did not bring any
[2] I told you I have a student ticket, didn't I?
[3] Who are you calling a punk?
[4] I told you my ticket got stolen. And so was my money. Leave

Making a disgusted gesture, the lad turns his attention back to counting chimneys.

The inspector turns all red and emotional: "Lost! Stolen! I have had it with you punks and your stupid excuses. You buy a ticket now or I will have the police take you out at the next stop!"
He reaches for the phone in his jacket.

The charged student jumps out of his seat right at the inspector. He stops inches away from his face and shouts: "Yeah! Yaouw mek me get off this train an' yaouw wull regret it, Oy swea. Police cawn does anythen. I wull find yaw fat asse an' boot it up into yow tonsils!"[5]

The inspector takes two steps back, trailed by the aggressor. They stop right next to my seat, the brawny athlete towering over the chubby inspector at least by a head.

"Don't you dare touch me…" squeaks the intimidated inspector. The fire head raises his fist and produces groaning sounds.

The delicate situation present itself to me as the opportunity I was looking for: "Can we not solve this peacefully?"

"What is it ter yaouw? yaouw stoy ert of this,"[6] yells the cornered kid in my direction without lowering his fist that still points at the inspector's nose.

---

me alone.
[5] You make me get off this train and you will regret it. Police cannot do anything. I will find you and kick your butt.
[6] What`s it to you? You stay out of this.

"I was thinking we could channel your energy into something more civilized than a brawl," I respond with an appeasing smile.

"That punk needs to buy a ticket" reminds the attacked authority, mustering up all his courage.

"Un mower toyme yaouw call me a poonk an' I wull pail yaouw up roight eya!"[7] viciously retaliates his opponent.

"I am prepared to pay for the young man's ticket." I suggest. "If he can beat me in an arm-wrestling match."

"You are joking, Sir?" suspects the inspector, his retracted head reemerging a bit from the collar of his humongous jacket.

"Oh, most certainly not."

"Why would you pay for this…?", he stops short of saying the 'p' word again, feeling the heat of the aggressor's breath and fist looming over him.

"Let's just say: I am trying to de-escalate a situation that looks to get out of hand."

I have been fantasizing about this kind of challenge many times. Whenever I see a guy with peaking biceps, I would love to wrestle this powerful arm. I have never actually challenged anyone to a match, of course. At least not anymore since 8th grade. I am not the kind of person who can pull this off like a natural buddies banter; like your everyday drinking contest. Even in adolescence, when

---

[7] One more time you call me a punk and I will beat you up right here

I first discovered this fantasy and the other guys my age were challenging the others, frolicking about all the time, I hardly ever managed to nonchalantly initiate an innocent test of strength. Latest after the age of thirty, only distinctively cool chaps could get away with it. But not me.

On top of my lack of cool, as a closeted gay man, I am always extra cautious even with the most transient physical contact with straight guys. I don't even pad shoulders.

Thus, this fantasy of mine is yet unfulfilled. Now I am far from home, the train is abandoned and I will meet none of the parties concerned ever again. Let's be a little daring for a change. I will see what happens as I go along.

"You want to buy another first-class ticket now?"

"Yes. Should our young friend here beat me in an arm-wrestling match."

Instead of jumping on the opportunity to get out of this alive, the authority under attack turns bossy and bureaucratic again, possibly as a means of self-affirmation: "I am afraid I do not have time for such games, Sir. Do you want to buy the ticket? Or not?"

"This bai guin ter tek lung"[8], smiles the young athlete, finding back to his cocky self.
"The goonz that almost pail yaouw up wull finish this aud geezer in not toyme"[9].
He raises both arms and contracts his biceps, looking at them in turn and smiling at me complacently.

"The young man has a point," I say. "Get me the ticket

---

[8] This is not going to take long.
[9] The arms that almost beat you up will finish this old man in not time.

FIRST CLASS FIRST TIME

and my unknown friend and I will sort this out later."

"What's the last stop?" the conductor asks me, as if I knew where my recent acquaintance was headed.

"Brighton" responds the lad without defocusing from his eye-catching arms.

The inspector prints the ticket and presents it to the lad. "I will take it for now, thank you", I say, snatching the ticket out of the invisible hand.

The lad leans over the inspector's face, grabbing him by

his lapels: "An noo leg it. An' mek sure I never see yaw stinken face agen or Oy boot yow asse up into yow tonsils!"[10]

The inspector hurries out of the coach as fast as he can, his big bum bouncing between the backrests like a pinball.

"Please join me", I point at the seat opposite me. The promoted first-class punk buoyantly slides onto the chair, now in a jolly mood.

He sizes me up in arrogant expectation. His arms don't look all that big when relaxed but as he warms himself up for the upcoming challenge by kneading his hands, on every twist the biceps jump up to a formidable size.

"What's your name?" I ask.

"Why d'ya care?"

"I just want to refer to you in some way. And I have to tell my friends who I took down today, don't I?" I tease the young athlete. "You don't want me to say, I beat some punk in a test of strength match today, do you?"

"Never in a rain of pigs pudding, bloke"[11], he contently replies, flexing his respect demanding muscles some more.

I assume his negation refers to me taking him down and not to him refusing to give me a name, so I try again: "You can tell me any name you like."

"Call me Nathan."

---

[10] And now go away. And make sure I never see your face again or I will kick your butt.
[11] This is never ever going to happen, bloke

"Is that your actual name?"

"It is me stage nerm."

"Stage name? What kind of stage?"

"Oy werk as a dancer sometoymes."

"Dancer as in ballet?" I smile.

"… or as in: Gogo?"

"Arr!"[12]

Presenting his muscles from different angles fully consumes him by now. This time I take it as being the answer to the second half of the question and try to figure out, how the obvious adoptability of my new friend in matters of moral chastity, earning money as a GoGo dancer, combined with his just as obvious deficits in perceptive faculty, can open up even more opportunities here.

Since I watched each episode of Peaky Blinders more than once, I can tell his accent is from Birmingham. My new friend would fit well in the cast of my favorite Netflix show, with his haircut and his attitude. He is just as simple-minded as most of its characters, it seems.

"That figures…," I continue, "I've never stayed in Birmingham. Maybe I should someday…? See you dance… by the way, my name is Robert."

Now I have his attention. You can see his brain working behind deadpan eyes, showing that my guess

---

[12] Yes!

regarding his decent was spot on. His ganglions seem to wrestle with how I could have known. He decides not to care, and I decide that watching his ganglions wrestle is not what I'm after.

"Shall we get started then," I break the silence.

"Started? With what?" The Birmingham thing had sent his brain into an infinity loop.

"Battle of the biceps! The arm-wrestling, remember? I was serious about this. You still have to earn the ticket."

"Whenever yaouw feel loike getten a pailin', bloke… I was born readay."

I take out my cuff links and roll up my sleeves. But the tailor-made shirt is too narrow. The lump of tight material wouldn't allow me to move my arms.
"This doesn't work. I will have to take it off," I comment and strip down to my t-shirt. I expect to impress him at least bit, since I am in excellent shape for an early thirties white collar guy. Yet he doesn't seem to notice, even though I am puffing up as much as possible.

"Oy saw yaouw gazen at me biceps all the toyme, yaouw know,"[13] the lad says.

"Oh, did you?"

"Yaouw were gawken all the toyme. Tryen ter 'oid behind yaw lickle notebook,"[14] he laughs.

---

[13] I saw you gazing at my biceps all the time, you know.
[14] You were staring all the time. Trying to hide behind your little notebook.

"Well, you have an impressive physique. I bet you invested a lot of time and potentially a substantial amount of cash on pharmaceutical substances into building it, didn't you? I guess you expect to be rewarded with serious admiration, don't you? And rightfully so, I may add."

He looks at me as if I am speaking Chinese.

"Well, then: let's see whether the t-shirt muscles are

just for show."

I place my elbow on the table in an arm-wrestling position. The lad grabs my hand and flexes his bicep again right away. Not to move my arm, but to show off. He looks at the mango-shaped muscle and smiles, exposing his tooth gap.

"Noo yaouw get a really close luke at them goonz. That is what yaouw wanted, eh?"[15]

To make sure he can't start a surprise attack, I apply some pressure. I work out quite regularly and when I do, I always train arms, so I hope to keep this competition going for a while; to get a close look at the young man's muscles at work, as he assumed; to experience their power.

"Am ya guin already? I doy fell anythen,"[16] the lad brags.

"Not yet. Wasn't sure if you're done posing!? Ready for some action, Brummie Boy?"

My young opponent now charges into the fight full steam ahead, expecting an easy win. He is damn strong and I panic a little. The show might be over much quicker than I was hoping.

Luckily my opponent continues to be more concerned with presenting his bicep than he is with the effect that it has on the competition. He still rather poses than tries to take me down, and that is just fine with me. For quite some time both of us stare at his bicep, our hands trembling from the power struggle.

---

[15] Now you get a really close look at the arms. This is what you wanted, isn't it?
[16] Are you going already? I don't feel anything.

After a while, though, my opponent decides that his ego will be even more pleased by putting me down fast now. With every second he does not make any progress Nathan's frustration grows, puzzled that his obvious physical superiority does not give him a decisive edge. Like a lot of muscle guys, though, Nathan has no clue how to wrestle arms properly. It is not pure strength. It is just as much technique. My confidence grows by holding my own for quite a while already.

Now Nathan intensifies his efforts again and I have to give a little. I pull his hand towards my chest and win back the lost territory. When Nathan reassembles his fiber army for another attack, I pull the base cap from his head and put it on mine backwards. My wide grin makes Nathan obviously very mad, but it also serves to distract him.

"I think I will end this now" I provoke Nathan even more.
"Naaa fuskin woy!"[17] Nathan squeezes out, half fearful, only half confident by now.
I use his momentary lack of concentration to put everything I got into a final move. With every inch he has to give, I gain momentum and a few seconds later Nathan's hand hits the tabletop.
I grin at Nathan jubilantly but he averts my eyes and throws himself back in his chair.

"It was the base cap, you see!?"
I don't think he gets the 'Over the top' movie reference.

Nathan kneads his sore muscle. "Yaouw got lucky. Did biceps to-die. Still bulloxed,"[18] he mumbles.

---

[17] No fucking way
[18] I am still tired

"Well, actually, I am left-handed, you know."

It is an outright lie, but it is just too much fun to add to his frustration and see the shock finally tanking his high spirit.

After a few minutes of silent joy on my part and groaning humiliation on Nathan's, I decide it is time to explore the further options to make this even better.

"Now we need to figure out your wager, don't we?"

"What the fock?"[19]

"My wager in our little bet was the ticket. In case you beat me. Which you didn't. We all witnessed that," I radiate a smug smile and let the offense sink in.

"We did not agree what your wager was."

Again, he looks at me as if I am speaking Chinese.

"Ok then. Shall we say: if I win, you let me touch your muscles?"

"Yaouw mean: touch me goonz?" Nathan speculates.

"For a start."

The young athlete welcomes this opportunity to regain his confidence, jumps up and throws the muscle right in my face. His arm is pumped with blood from the hard work it just had to do, so the vein on top of his peaked bicep looks like it's about to burst. Nathan marvels at his own muscles just as much as I do and, in an instant,

---

[19] What the fuck

certainty of superiority supersedes the humiliation.

I put my hand on top of the peak and squeeze it; touch and feel from every angle; wrap both hands around his arm and squeeze more.

"Wow!" I utter to cheer him into further action.
He opens and closes his elbow. The muscles bulging under my palms send electric ants up and down my spine.

"What about the other one? Is it just as big?"

The lad casually hits a double biceps pose and then presents his left arm. I inspect that just as diligently.

Now Nathan is on a roll. He flexes both arms right under my nose, tightening the rest of his torso. My hands run up and down the arms; then travel up to the shoulders; one hand continues the journey toward his chest. I'm so surprised and excited by this opportunity that I lose all reservations. My fingertips explore the gorge between the two massive lumps. Nathan's eyes follow my hands exploring his chiseled body. He does not seem bothered at all; just pleased with the excited reaction to his accomplishments.
He gasps for air, straightens his back and squeezes his palms against each other while tensing every fiber in his upper body. He reaches for the seam of his shirt and stretches the garment until you hear tearing sounds. I gawk at the cleavage down to the happy trail. He drops back and lifts his shirt for an even better view at his amazing abs.

"Yaouw loike those?"[20]

My very obvious delight encourages him to take the

---

[20] You like those?

shirt off and continue the show. I half way climb onto the tabletop to open the presents.

After a while Nathan drops back in his seat, exhausted.

"Got what yaouw wanted?"

"That was absolutely stunning, thank you. You have a splendid body."

"Oy knoo guys loike yaouw" he says after quite a few more deep breaths.

"Guys like me?"

"Faggits."

The term hits me right in the gut. Somehow it had not even occurred to me that my excitement and such indulgence in haptic curiosity would of course trigger this diagnosis. I got carried away.
I remind myself that I will never meet Nathan again. It is irrelevant what he thinks. And it's too exciting to stop now.

"You mean men fascinated by the male physique!?"

"Whatever."

"You have gay friends?"

"Hell no!"
"They are me subscroibers."

"Subscribers?"

"On me Onlyfans page."

"Your what?", I play innocent.

"Oy yav a webpage on the net. On Onlyfans. I post pictures an' videos. People subscroibe ter see them. I yav loads of subscroibers."

"They pay money to see videos of you? What kind of videos?"

"Just loike this here. Oy flex. Sometoymes Oy film me workout. Stuff loike that."

"How much do people pay for that privilege?"

"Ten pounds a month. The'er is a discount ter 5 pounds in case yoo miskin interested," he smirks.

"People pay ten pounds for videos of you flexing? Every month?"

"Arr! Oy yam the bostin'. Fuskin bostin' body on the net."[21]

"Well, you have a magnificent body, that's for sure. But, I mean, you just show off your hard earned muscles? That's it?"

"Oy send them special videos, too. They can wetch fer nineteen pounds."

"Nineteen pounds for one video? Wow! What do I get to see for nineteen pounds?"

"Yoo miskin not getten ter see anythen. Yaouw got

---

[21] Yes! I am the best. The fucking best body on the net.

what yaouw wanted. Gid me me ticket."[22]

My young companion does not seem to appreciate where this debate is headed.

I need to revise Nathan's preliminary profile. The fat bully victim got all brawny and discovered he can get a lot of admiration now. All this admiration turns nagging self-doubt into narcissism. In revenge for the pain inflicted on him, he now looks down on his submissive subscribers that remind him of his former insecure self. Everybody he meets is just a worshipper that deserves to be mistreated. To admire his body will not make him like me back. I need to provoke him to takes this any further.

"Oh, my dear friend. This is a misunderstanding. The brief show I got was the price for you losing the match. We haven't even talked about the price for the ticket."

There it is once more: that bewildered look on the young lad's face.

"You see: When I say, I buy you a ticket, when I lose, I don't have to buy it, when I win. Correct? You still owe me the ticket, I say."

"Yaouw got yaw acker's worth of a shoo roight eya, Oy say!"[23] Nathan exclaims with more than a slight aggression in his voice.

"Come on! That ticket must have paid for a couple of months subscription plus specials."
"What do you do in those special videos, anyway?"

---

[22] You are not getting to see anything. You got what you wanted. Give me my ticket.
[23] You got your money's worth of a show right here, I say.

While he still stares me down, the young aggressor's squinted eye slits after a while cease firing thunderbolts. Then his gaze turns more introspective and eventually his expression morphs from hostility to boaster pride and his eyes sparkle in joyful anticipation.

"Regular subscriber gets them goonz. If yaouw booy the special yow get this!" The lad opens button and zipper of the jeans, shoves his pants down, pulls his shirt up and slabs his huge, meaty penis on the tabletop. This thing is bigger in relaxed condition than most weenies are when fully erect.

"Jesus..." I utter in awe, "What a monster", feeling embarrassed for not finding anything more ingenious to say to buy me some time. I hadn't expected him to actually respond to my teasing; at least not so fast. The proud proprietor rolls the succulent sausage on the tabletop from left to right with two fingers.

After I recover a bit from the pleasant surprise, I continue the teasing: "You are saying you masturbate on cam?"

"Oy wank meself all the toyme anywoy" he says, as if this explains why he sells videos of his most intimate actions to other people. This attitude opens up exceptional opportunities for this to continue, though.

He drops back to his seat.

I pull over my notebook, turn it around and point the screen at him: "let's pretend this is your web cam. What do you do next?" It is a longshot, I know, but worth a try.

The lad eyeballs me again for what feels like an eternity. You can see the cogwheels of a mechanical brain behind blank eyes work through the possible responses.

Suddenly, his focus shifts to the coach door.

RICHARD T. GRAYSON

FIRST CLASS FIRST TIME

"That bloody inspector weasels abart in the anunst coach," he hisses, "ee is tryen ter see what is guin on."[24]

"Don't worry," I try to calm Nathan "He cannot see you got your pants down. The important bits are all covered."

"When Oy get ard they eynt, trussen me,"[25] he grins.

"This numpty does not tell me what ter does anyway!"[26] he shouts as if he wants the inspector to hear it in the next coach.
It looks as if his rule breaker instinct is about to get the best of him. I can see the adrenalin kick in.

Nathan pulls the lever to recline his backrest, kicks off his shoes and puts his feet against my seat. One foot he places between my legs, his toes teasing my erect dick. That almost hurts, particularly as my erection has been fighting for space in my tight trousers ever since we locked hand for the match.

"Seems loike yoo miskin ready", Nathan smirks, leans back, and begins to jerk his meaty prick.

The lad strokes the thick stick with one hand while the other massages his pecs. He pushes his pelvis up to stick his cock out above the tabletop. Holding this acrobatic bridged position while fondling his strained muscles instantly arouses Nathan. His dick grows to ten inches, surely. I don't dare to reach out to touch his torso, and I don't want to touch his hardon. I settle for watching the

---

[24] The inspector weasels about in the next coach. He is trying to see what is going on here.
[25] When I get hard they are not, trust me.
[26] And this simple minded person does not tell me what to do anyway

show while petting his strained, shivering thighs and calves under the table.

In his self-indulgence, the young renegade has not forgotten about his audience. And his intended audience is not just me. He gets up and takes a long grim look down the coach isle. It is obvious Nathan wants the ticket inspector to see this. I don't know if this time he has a plan what he would do if the object of his loathing enters our coach, but in my fantasy I picture the muscled athlete exploding right in the face of the podgy pesterer and chasing him down the aisle, while shooting load after load at him. Seems both of us are getting carried away again.

Nathan leans forward, supports himself on the table and jerks his stick ever faster. The more frantic he strokes, the tighter his muscles become. He gasps for air and moans.

Nathan's breathing turns to panting and the moaning to whimpering. The lad is clearly about to come. He drops back into the chair and lifts his pump gun above the tabletop again. He lets out a loud groan and shoots his salute all the way up to the ceiling lights. Most of the cum from six blasts rains down on the table, missing my notebook by an inch. Some hits his abs.

The exhausted masturbator slumps down with a deep sigh.

"Wow!" I say, "I'd buy that video. That was quite a load!".

I pass Nathan a pack of tempos. He takes out half of them, cleans his abs and drops them on the table without swiping up the mess he made there.

He crouches in his chair empty faced catching his breath.

After a short while the cogwheels in his brain resume rotation and since his erection has eased off, he pulls his pants up and slides into his shoes.

"Gid me me ticket noo!" he commands, while he puts the shirt back on.

I don't want to let it end just yet.

"Well... you know... this was good and all... but as you already noted, this got me all excited... what do you think I should do now?"

"Oy fink yaouw should gid me the fuskin ticket noo!"[27] Nathan exclaims in a very serious voice.

"You don't get it," I hear myself say, "I have a raging hardon that needs attention." My audacity shocks me.

"Naaa woy!" Nathan yells, jumping up. "Oy told yaouw Oy a no faggit!"[28]

"You owe me. Your ticket is at least the price of four of your special videos". It could be arousal or angst that

---

[27] I think you should give me my fucking ticket now.
[28] I told you I am not faggot

makes me shake. I rather stay seated for now; my knees might be too weak to stand my ground.

"I doe owe yaouw anythen," Nathan shouts.

"So, you agree you do owe me!?"
It's obvious he doesn't get the double negative witticism. He does get, though, that I am wisecracking him. He evidently hates that.

"Doy odge it!"[29] Nathan says with an irritatingly restrained, thus even more intimidating tone, sitting down again and getting very close, pointing at my face, his hand formed to a gun.
"Yaouw got paid enough, Oy say."

"It is a fucking first-class ticket we are talking about! I can get three blow jobs for that kind of cash in Paddington any time," I explain with a cracking voice, trying to hold my own. It's worth a try, I reckon.

Nathan sinisterly stares me down from only inches away for endless heartbeats hammering in my head. I only just manage to not flinch.

"It is a fuskin fust class ticket alrooight. An' noo yaouw fink yaouw get a fust class fuskin in return, ey?"[30] is the pretty canny response he comes up with. He leans back and laughs a very dirty laugh, obviously just as surprised by his wit as I am.

"Tek dowl them trousers," Nathan commands.

---

[29] Don´t push it
[30] It is a fucking first class ticket alright. And now you think you will get a first class fucking in return, don't you?

I open my belt and do as I am told. Nathan disappears under the table. His warm hand grabs my raging erection, the other my balls. I lean back and close my eyes in exited expectation.

My knees hit the table full force when I convulse as a reflex to the intense pain Nathan causes by squashing my balls. I scream in agony.

"Stop! Let go!" I shout, but he doesn't. Instead, he pulls my balls as if he is trying to rip them off.

I throw myself back and forth in intense pain, not even able to go for his hands.

Nathan squeezes on for eternal seconds before he releases his grip. He creeps out from underneath the table, hovers over me and drops a mean straight jab right on my jaw.

"Oy warned yaouw not ter odge it, didn't Oy?" he hisses.

As the blur clears, Nathan stands in the aisle laughing: "See what I got eya. Yaw wallet. An me ticket. Looks loike that yaw hardon is tayken care of as well." He grins at my tormented tinder stick.

I want to jump after him, reaching for my pants, trying to pull them up while getting out of the seat, tripping over them and stumbling in the aisle, bumping straight into Nathan. His knee hits my face full force and I fall over. My balls hurt, and so does my jaw and nose. I lie on my back and look up to Nathan, who kicks me in the gut one more time.

"Tarra!"[31]

He turns around, puts on his backpack, grabs the hoody and leaves towards the door. I realize the train had come to a halt.

---

[31] See you around

CHERRY BLOSSOM

First time in an Onzen

To accompany your boss on a trip halfway around the world to Tokyo for important negotiations is hard enough. Being new to the job and, moreover, being new to any job, makes it a grueling task. To prepare for this trip I had received cultural awareness training, so I knew that, in dealing with Japanese, losing face was the second worst thing you could do. The only thing even worse was making somebody else lose face. The balancing act of trying to impress my boss by being clever but not to offend or just belittle any of our Japanese hosts ad kept me extremely tensed up all day. After ten long hours of negotiations, only outrages levels of adrenalin and endorphins keep me from collapsing.

On the way back to our accommodation, my boss complements me on how I have been holding up. His feedback means a lot to me since my boss is famous in the feed-the-hungry-shelter-the-homeless-scene of global NGOs for his negotiation skills. He can get decision makers, in governments and private corporations alike, to do things they would have never imagined doing; especially when it comes to donating money for charitable causes.

He says it's because he can read people's minds. Discover their genuine desires. What makes them tick? What their hidden agendas and ultimate motivations are? How to win them over, tempt them, lure them? What to offer them to be their friend?

He says I had proven to him today that he was right from the start regarding my potential; that he has detected already in our job interview that there is a distinct talent in me as well for this kind of mind reading. More endorphins kick in. The next thing I should learn, though, is to understand myself. To be successful in the bargaining game, it's equally important, he says, to know one's own genuine wishes. The hidden agenda of one's own sub conscience. Only then, others cannot manipulate you in the same way that you try to influence them. I cannot completely follow his train of thought, but the one thing I do get is I am now enrolled in a special negotiator training program by one of the best in the business. And that excites me a lot.

My boss says Japanese are the toughest. For one, because they show no emotion; never react on impulse; are always restrained. And it was true. All day long we had looked at stony masks with barely ever any facial expressions. As if it wasn't difficult enough to read faces that look so different from what you are used to that you cannot even guess their age. No wonder Japanese invented the robots, I thought after the first hour of our meeting. They even use fewer gestures than R2D2.

Only on karaoke nights, with lots of hard booze, the masks would fall off. But here the consensus seems to be: everybody gets wasted and nobody remembers a thing the next day. So it does not matter. I will find out about it, I guess, when we go for karaoke night with our hosts at the end of the week.

The second reason for the Japanese mastership in bargaining is that, because of the permanent self-control of everybody around them, they are excellently trained to detect and interpret even the faintest signs. For them we are an open book, and what our spontaneous reactions will not tell them, we will give away by trying so hard to open them up and build some rapport that we just keep on talking. In no other country is it so hard to bargain, my boss says.

During the negotiations of today, he had used a petty trick. Once, every so often, at the most awkward of occasions, he dropped a quote on our hosts. Not a quote from a philosopher or poet. He used quotes from Yoda, the Yedi.

This confused our counterparts big time. They just couldn't figure out what to make of this. Did he believe Yoda was a thinker worth taking guidance from? In the same league as Laotse and Konfuzius, who, even though they were Chinese, they could potentially accept as a source of sound advice on life. Or did he quote Yoda ironically, as you quote, say, Oskar Wild? Or, worst of all, did he look down on them by insinuating that they appreciate Yoda as a proper philosopher?

Not all the words of wisdom he dished out throughout the day were even actual quotes of Yoda. He made them up as he went along, matching the typical Yoda style of speaking but with content that fitted to the point he was trying to make. It was safe to do so, because early on it became apparent that our hosts were not all that familiar with Yoda's oeuvre.

When you are not sure whether you must treat your opponent like an idiot, a genius, a scallywag or anything in between, you cannot manipulate him to where you need him to be. Your enemy know you must. Only then, fight you can.

It has been impressive to observe and quite effective. We already are much closer to having them set up a generously funded charity foundation than we expected to be after the first meetings.

My boss had filled me in on this technique he intended to use on our flight into Tokio. I thought it was a joke at first. Especially since he gave me a t-shirt to commemorate my first long-distance trip that showed a picture of Yoda and a genuine quote: "On many long journeys I have gone and waited for others to return from theirs. Some do. Some are broken. And some come back so different, only their names remain."

This remarkable man knows his way around most parts of the world. Listening to his travel stories, he must have been to half the UN member nations. Even though he is only in his mid-thirties. He heads up the U.S. office of the law firm they hired me into straight out of law school a few months ago. And he coordinates the law firm's pro-bono activities for the United Nations.

To read the minds of people, you have to understand their culture. That's why my boss puts great emphasis on the extracurricular activities of our trip and tells me endless stories about his travels. In particular, from his earlier trips to Japan. He treats me in a patronizing way, but I enjoy the special attention I am getting and appreciate the guidance of a man of his caliber and experience. Since it's my first trip to the country, he wants me to experience as much of the Japanese particularities as possible, he says. The law firm's founding partners are wealthy philanthropists, with a weak spot for cultural exchange and a high regard for the result my boss achieves with his approach, so this trip's budget is generous, to say the least.

We are not staying in one of these cloned business hotels in the Shinjuku station area. My boss had chosen a traditional 'Ryokan' instead. These small family run places provide an excellent introduction to Japanese culture, since you sleep on tatami pads on the floor instead of proper boxsprings and they treat you with an authentic set Japanese style breakfast and not the usual international buffet. Our new home is tugged away in a shielded courtyard and surrounded by cherry trees, and since it is cherry blossom season, you could not get more iconically Japanese than this.

My boss was particularly praiseful about the traditional Japanese bathing experience of an Onzen. Since the old days an Onzen combined public bath house and relaxation retreat. Originally built as outdoor facilities at hot springs, the water containing distinctive minerals and the calm atmosphere promise maximum relaxation. Most Ryokans prides themselves for providing indoor, yet otherwise very traditional versions of this experience. This means stringent etiquette on bathing attire, as in: nude, and on hygiene, as in: sterilizing diligence in cleaning yourself.

The implicit suggestion of a joint visit to the Onzen in our Ryokan was more special attention than I felt inclined to put up with, though. I am not sure what makes me more uncomfortable: The thought of being in the buff in front of my boss? Seeing my superior buck naked? Or being seen as an uptight drag if I refused to come along? The lasting effect either of these options may have on our working relationship concerned me big time.

In tutorials for job interviews I had heard about special advice for confrontational situations or stress tests: to picture your opposition naked. It takes out the tension of the argument and helps you regain control. To take offenses seriously is hard when they are coming from a naked guy. How do you take your boss seriously ever again once you have actually seen him stripped?

So I was glad my boss called it an early night after a rushed dinner, because they expect us back at our business partner offices the next morning at 7.30 o'clock.

My adrenalin level is still up, though, from the intense talks of today and all the emotions of this trip. A brochure in my room explaining the Onzen tradition sparks my curiosity again, so I wonder if such a meditative experience may help me refocus for the next morning. It is a terrible time anyway to call my girlfriend in Seattle, where it's 4 a.m., so I decide to give the Onzen ceremony a try, hoping to score brownie points with my boss when I tell him about it at breakfast.

He had admonished me quite often to open my mind for novel adventures. He calls me 'farm boy' ever since I told him about my upbringing in the Great Plains and that I was dating the same girl since junior high. One reason I wanted this job was I want to see the world. Considering all this doesn't leave me a choice.

The brochure outlines the strict Onzen protocol in all details, so foreigners cannot make too many mistakes. The closet provides house slippers and a daringly short Kimono, looking goofy on a six foot two American. I had rejected the suggestion to wear this attire for the breakfast ceremony but it seems just fine for the pool. I grab a towel and find my way to the Onzen area, where, to my great relief, I'm alone in the compact dressing room while I strip naked, following the instructions from the brochure. I deposit my stuff in a cabinet, which to my surprise does not even have a lock.

Sauna is not my cup of Matcha, because the altar boy in me is very uncomfortable being naked around other people; not just my superiors. And my curiosity for fresh adventures is most often rather academic than aimed at making practical experiences. Not knowing what to expect behind the frosted glass door frightens me. From the bright dressing room the pool area seems like a dark dungeon. As I pull the door open, hot steam hovers my way.

Upon entering my roll call registers two older men in the pool and two more showering at the side of the space before I even realize the beautifully illuminated Zen garden behind a top-to-bottom glass wall at the back of the room. The washing spots are not in a separate room but on opposite walls both sides of the pool. They are equipped with miniature shower seats that looks like they come straight from a nursery for three-year-olds.
The locals mind their own affairs and ignore the foreigner. I don't mind at all and rush to one of the dollhouse stools. An adult my size can hardly sit on the tiny piece of furniture, but at least the stooped and cowered posture supports my attempt to be invisible.

In order to not pollute the hot water pool, the protocol mandates to cleanse yourself extremely diligently before entering. It is impossible for a tall and clumsy Westerner not to look ridicules when trying to soap up in this preschool sized setting. Especially since the showerhead is plugged to a hosepipe so short, I can hardly reach all parts of my body with this torturing device.

Since any attempt to be elegant is useless under these circumstances, I just do my best to demonstrate utmost hygiene; I soap and wash every part of my body at least three times; I make sure the two men already showering finish up way before me; only then I declare this phase of the ritual completed. There is yet another very important part of the Onzen liturgy to be performed, though, as outlined in the brochure, which is spilling one last bucket of clean water over my head before I can walk over to the hot pool.

The pool measures about fifteen times twenty feet and is only a little over two feet deep, with two stair steps leading to the ground along the full stretch of both long sides. The four old men sit on the floor of the pool, facing the Zen garden, resting their elbows on the top step.

One reason for the tradition to be naked in an Onzen, my boss had explained to me, is that you could not hide any weapons back in the days when it was still custom behavior to carry armament. Since I sense to be in enemy territory with the four geezers ignoring me in a hostile way, I decide to follow an old tradition where I come from, to never sit with the back to the Saloon door. I enter at the very end of the opposite side, facing the entrance. Nobody will come in or leave without me taking notice.

The old men disregard my greeting and talk in such soft voices amongst themselves that it's impossible to understand a word from a few feet away, even if it wouldn't be in Japanese. I pretend to be consumed by the ritual and try to focus on what I am here for: relaxation. Two minutes later, though, I get an idea what they might have been talking about. In a coordinated effort, the four leave the pool. My diligent washing routine obviously did not convince them I decontaminated myself properly, and that it was safe to share the hot pool with this impure alien. I am offended; inclined to comment on this ignorance; but then opt to enjoy that I will now have the hot pool to myself.

FIRST CLASS FIRST TIME

The four seniors repeat a condensed version of the cleaning ritual, also an important part of the Onzen ceremonies, before they leave for the dressing room. I can see the shadows of their crooked, scrawny old bodies as silhouettes projected on the frosted glass door by the locker room's bright ceiling lights.

The hot, mineral-nourished water feels relaxing yet kind of draining and I am already dizzy. Just as I want to close my eyes, I notice another silhouette on the frosted glass. This time the tensed posture indicates a younger man and as he turns towards the slide door to open it, the silhouette shows what looks like a Tanto sword dangling from his hip. I rest my head on the poolside and observe only through the slits of my eyes when the shadow enters. What if that guy meets the expectations raised by his silhouette? Lord, please, do not have me encounter such temptation, being helplessly exposed in this hot pool.

My prayers are ignored.

Instead of facing the wall when crouching on the little stool, like everybody else, the intruder sits cross-legged facing the room. From the corner of my eyes the young Asian looks like he is about my age, with handsome, boyish features and a freakish, semi-long, Anime hair style. His athletic body is ultra-ripped. And his California roll is definitely a full lunch.

The handsome Hondo hunk starts the showering ritual by first ruining his Anime spikes and then drizzling water on the rest of his amazing body. When he moves, his muscles tense; and when they tense, you can see every single fiber string the muscle composes of underneath almost transparent skin. The guy looks like a walking anatomy chart in biology class.

FIRST CLASS FIRST TIME

Manga boy soaps himself up with a slim towel. One muscle at a time. Counting the fibers. The intruder moves in elegant, fluid motions. While massaging the foam into each fiber individually, he twists and turns his body, presenting his best angles. The soap coated, tensed muscles glisten even in the dim light.

Immersed into beholding this display of physical perfection, I notice blood pulsing into my crotch. This pulls me out of my state of trance just in time; this very moment, the guy looks straight my way. I transiently catch his Manga eyes glowing like those of a cat in the dark while I instantaneously close the blinds and pretend to be meditating.

When I hear the wooden stool being pushed across the floor, I dare to glance over again, finding the guy standing upright, leaning with his back against the tiled wall. Just as slowly as he had soaped himself up, he now rinses the foam off with the thin stream of water pouring from the shower head. Manga guy twists and turns his perfect physique again in just as perfect poses, tensing his muscles as if this was an adult art photo shoot. While he is posing, his meaty pecker bobs back and forth and left and right in slow motion.

At the very end of the cleansing ritual, the shredded athlete sits down again because the hose is not long enough to reach his backside while standing. This time he faces the wall. As the trickling water rinses off the foam, it unveils an opulent and colorful tattoo that ornaments his wingy back. The ink art shows a dragon, a snake and a tiger, framed by stylized flowers, symbolizing chrysanthemums, lotuses and cherry blossoms, I guess. The drawing in the center shows a weird mask.

I recall that my boss had explained to me that in former times tattoos were frowned upon in Japanese society because they were most prevalent in organized crime circles. In Onzens and public bath houses Yakuza members and thus tattoos were banned and another reason for the custom to be naked when entering an Onzen is to not be able to hide a tattoo, no matter how petite it was. Even today, the story continued, it's unusual in Japan to have a tattoo that is visible when dressed. Different to the trends in the western world, to proclaim one's life philosophy publicly thru ostentatious ink, Japanese consider tattoos a private pleasure. It is ironic, my boss concluded, that showing off Yakuza motif tattoos became so popular in the U.S. in recent years.

This extensive narration had started when my boss asked me if I had any kind of tattoo on me. I found being interrogated on my body adornments just as inadequate as sharing a hot pool with my boss. He sensed my discomfort with the subject and went on to explain that one reason he had picked our Ryokan was its very traditional Onzen. Like most traditional Onzens, though, it still today does not welcome guests with tattoos.

The opulent tattoo on Manga guy could well be a Yakuza motif. But if it is, he must be new to the firm, because they usually get their entire body inked, I recall from the Yakuza movies I have seen. This guy still has a lot of unchartered ground on the rest of his body, I lull myself, so at least he is not a veteran killer. As if being the first ever victim is only half as bad.
Just as my mind wants to start evolving this storyline, after the final bucket swoop, the aspiring assassin walks over to the pool and places himself on the top stair step opposite me.
I cross my legs to hide my more than semi-firm dick. The water is crystal clear and only tiny ripples on the surface impair the view. If it wasn't for the dim lighting, my arousal would surely have been noted immediately.

FIRST CLASS FIRST TIME

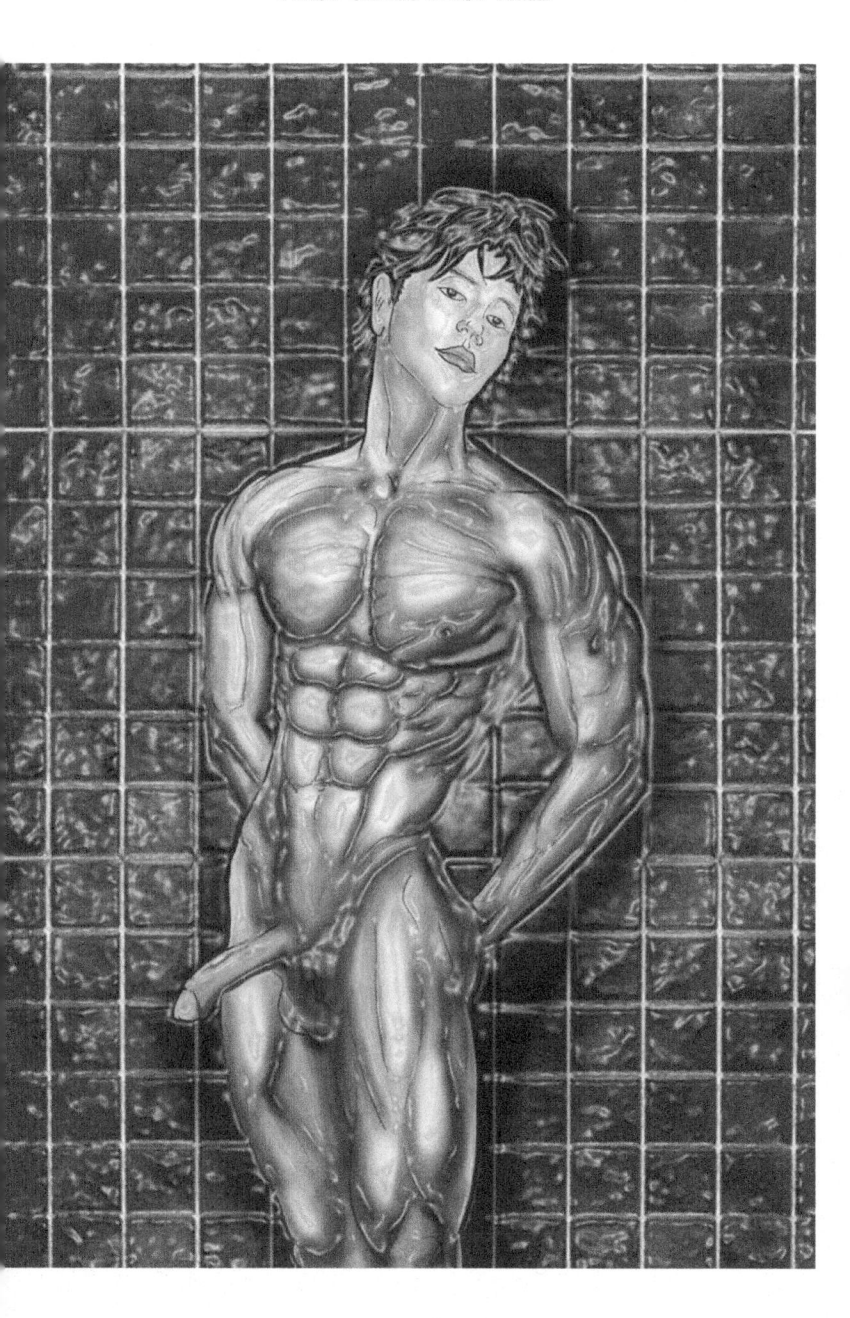

I try not to stare too blatantly but still can't resist scanning the details of the vascular and perfectly sculptured physiques just a few feet away. He folds up the small towel he used for washing, puts it on his forehead and leans back. To reverse the blood flow in my groin, I try concentrating on something else. Anything.

Simply bolting this awkward situation is no option, since I can't step out of this pool while my excitement is still so obvious. I lay my head back and close my eyes.

May the force be with me.

'Your first time?' the Anime assassin asks in perfect, accent free English. I feel caught out. After a few seconds, though, my dizzy brain determines that the question rather relates to the hot pool experience.

"Yeah" I utter, not even looking. I can sense him smirking.

"The key thing is: Relax and enjoy. But whatever you do: Don't pollute the water."

Now I do look, thinking what this could mean and if I needed to react somehow. The guy still sits on the top stair step, but now in a full split. Like all his poses before, also the full split is perfectly executed. Through the smooth surface, I see his tremendous cock dangling halfway down to the ground of the pool. I want to look away, but can't. And I don't have to, because the ultra-lean athlete doesn't take notice of me anymore. He leans forward and chips water onto his arms and shoulders. From this close, the ropey muscle cords underneath the shimmering skin appear even more unreal. Next he leans back and scoops water onto his torso to watch it finding its way down the tiled midsection. He repeats this a few times, each time tensing different slabs on the carved chute creating a unique form of cataract. The next scoops he shovels onto his stringy chest with both hands, stopping it from running straight down and accompanying it with a hand barrier all the way along the abs alley.

The athlete sits up straight, relaxes his tension, lowers his head and closes his eyes. I gasp for air the first time after what feels like minutes. The reason for my windedness meditates motionlessly for quite a while and even in this relaxed state countless striations are carved into each muscle. He looks just like the Dragon Ball Son Goku action figures I had bought as a souvenir in one of Tokio's multi-story Manga shops.

I sit as still as I can and try not to breathe. The smoother the surface becomes, the better view I get at Goku's now semi-erect monkey tail pointing out at a ninety-degree angle; steadily rising.

While his muscular body is molded after the martial arts fighter, his face is the archetype of a leading man in a Manga romance. Stunningly handsome, with almond eyes and a small and slender European style nose. Only the full lips do not follow manga standards. But most amazing is the complexion of his skin. Manga boy's thin skin covering his ripped to shreds muscles is already quite silky. Yet the face almost seems photoshopped on the wiry torso. It is so smooth it doesn't even seem to have pores at all. Mannequin dolls have more structure on their skin than this pearly, perfectly polished face. Even the skin tones of cheeks and chest do not match, as if he was still wearing make-up after the diligent cleansing routine.

My open-mouthed musing about the work of art in front of me ends abruptly when the dragon comes alive again and inhales deeply. He leans his head back and so do I. His hands start caressing his inner thighs and I keep watching cautiously, always prepared to change focus. As his hands circle the tear drop shaped muscles, the strained fiber bundles of his chest seem to be trying to rip the sternum apart and when they move towards his groin, his pecs swell up and mount at his cleavage, forming a deep gorge. Yet the athlete doesn't even seem to be flexing at all. It is just what meaty muscles look like when only covered by the thinnest of skins, I reckon.

And this is what a hardon ready to explode looks like, I realize as I look down on myself.

On every round trip of caressing his thighs, Goku inhales and exhales in the same slow rhythm. My mind searches for something to think that will ease the excitement and allow me to escape. All it comes up with, though, is the question, why Asian men often have unproportionally massive chests? The simultaneously inflating rib-cage and pectoral muscles on my pool companion are an otherworldly sight. I realize that I am staring at them like a thirteen-year-old gazes at the first tits he ever gets to touch. Then again: these are the first man boobs of that quality I am exposed to in actual life; and how much I yearn touch them.

The meditating martial artist now engages in slow, fluid, wide range, tai-chi gestures. He focusses on his pointing fingers extended out in front of his sternum, exhales, strains all muscles in his torso, relaxes again and floats his hands up and down. Then he presses the palms against each other and circles them around in front of his torso while I parse the hundreds of wire rope hoists underneath the transparent skin orchestrate the motions.
Countless Cords and strings pull and wind the extremities into various tai-chi postures in smooth, circling flows, opening and closing the arms, swinging them left to right or up and down, sometimes tensed, sometime eased.

I gaze hypnotized at the performance when suddenly the

door from the dressing room slides open. An old man walks in. Tai-chi boy acknowledges the intrusion in his back just by lifting a brow without even opening an eye and continues with his mediation untroubled. His routine now alternates between simulated, slow motion punch moves, tensed muscle poses and stretch positions he may execute a little more aggressively than before yet seemingly unfazed by worries to get caught with a growing hardon.

The old man extends a cursory greeting at us without even glancing in our direction and walks over to the first shower seat. From his position the Manga fighter's body should shield both our excitement from the old man's eyes, I trust, especially in this dim light and from this distance. However, this will only help until he finishes his shower and enters the pool.

The old man is about to commence the cleaning procedure. Just a guy in a full split on the stair step of a pool exercising seated tai-chi may not cause too much attention. It is Japan, mind you, and these people engage in many weird rituals. But as the old man takes a longer look, he freezes, starring at the Anime athlete's artfully inked back.

It could just be the tattoo that puts him off. Yet maybe he considers the meditation exercises of the tattooed fighter to be the preparation for a ritual Yakuza killing about to take place. That would certainly pollute the sacred water, I giggle. Whatever it is, the old man escapes the future crime scene as fast as he had appeared.

The inked assassin lifts an eyebrow again, relaxes his tensed body and starts massaging his pecs, gradually working his way down to his tightening abs. Then he supports his weight on his elbows and puts back his head. Meanwhile, his manhood has grown to full size telescoping way above water level like a submarine look-out aiming at me. I do not dare to touch my throbbing tool as I fear it would instantly explode. 'Whatever you do, don't pollute the water' rings his voice in my head.

While my panicking mind still ponders on a distraction, to make my erection ease off, Manga guy gasps loudly. He tenses and relaxes his eight pack in slow, rhythmic, rolling motions, contracting and relaxing each row of tiles sequentially from bottom to top and then from top to bottom. Next, he adds a circling motion of his pelvis to the waves of contractions. His breathing frequency increases and so does the sound level.

With his hands behind his head, he moves as if he is working out his abs. After a few repetitions, with a deep gasp of air, he vacuums his tummy up into his rib-cage. His midsection is now as thin as a tatami mat. It looks as if I could reach right in from the bottom and grab his heart. It makes me wonder if his inner organs have now been sucked up inside his chest since the rib-cage has doubled in volume.

As he expels the air from his chest, the inner organs seem to sag back down again. It now looks like his abdominal plates are armoring a pumpkin. In a slow pulse he continues to vacuum in and push out his abs in rolling repetitions. On every cycle he flexes a unique part of his midsection. This Hokkaido hard body seems to control every muscle fiber in his body individually.

With his pelvis rolled up, his sperm spitter is aimed back at himself like a rocket launcher. He inhales deeply again, opens his eyes and peers hard at me, smiling. I am frozen. In the very second he releases the air and tenses his abs with a suppressed moan his gigantic semen gun is triggered and discharges a huge white load that hits him right in the face. He doesn't even blink. A second one lands on his pecs, the following one on his abs. The explosive eruptions make his body writhe. Yet he still manages to control the aim of his wad launcher. The third and fourth load also rain down on his abs. Not one drop lands in the water.

He puffs, looks down on his speckled torso, beams at his enormous ejaculator, wipes the last drops from the tip and licks it off his finger. This is the first time during this entire routine he touches his tool.

After a few moments gasping for air, he pushes himself up to the poolside and rises to walk over to the showers.

While he cleans himself, my rotating mind checks options again. Should I just run out even though every motion could push me over the edge? I am not too worried anymore that my Yakuza friend would realize my excitement; he may well have already noted that; but what if somebody back in the dressing room sees my erect penis before I can dress back up? I am not even sure the short

Kimono properly covers my sword. The embarrassment would be unbearable.

Yet, what if I stay and the next guy comes in here? Would it be possible to hide my erection for long enough for it to ease off? The washing ceremony would take a few minutes before he would enter the pool. The light is dim. I picture myself splashing up the surface to obstruct the view, but that seems inappropriately cheerful for the serious Onzen liturgy.

Anyway, I decide to stay under water for now. With the auto-climaxing athlete the allure will soon be gone, I will meditate the attraction away, my arousal will ease and all will be fine.

Nicely cleaned up but still pretty firm, Manga boy walks straight back to the pool, steps inside and sits himself right next to me on the lower stair step. He leans back and closes his eyes, paying no attention to me and my confusion.

I am stunned by the nerve of this guy. How can he not get out of here as fast as possible after what he just did?

In the absence of any better plan, I close my eyes as well and try not to think of his meaty pecs, his beautiful face, his amazing abs or his super-size, zero-touch tool.

When you look at the dark side, careful you must be. For the dark side looks back.

Lord, let this be over soon.

Just as I almost convinced myself this was only a weird dream, I sense something touching my cock. The blood just on its way out changes direction at once. Fingers softly massage my cherry and pet the shaft. My confused mind double checks all channels to confirm it's not my hand acting on my daydream.

RICHARD T. GRAYSON

FIRST CLASS FIRST TIME

Unable to react, I let it happen, frantically trying to think straight. As the stroking gets more intense, I reach for the hand to stop it and turn over to my tormentor.

To my surprise, the space next to me is vacant. Instead, Manga boy sits right in front of me on the floor of the pool in a full split again with just his head above the surface. His glowing eyes beam at me. I indignantly stare back a silent 'Stop!' and grab his wrist.

He slowly rises from the water, still clinging on to my dick, massaging it by tightening and loosening the grip.

He leans in on me. I push back. The smoothly coated muscles ripple and bulge under my touch. I can sense the enormous power these fibers could summon up. He grabs my wrists and guides my hands across his strained torso, and when he advances further, I put up on only half-hearted resistance. He reaches for my neck and gently pulls me closer. Under my palms his pulsating pecs comprising bundled ropes wrapped in shimmering silk inflate to the volume of honeydew melons.

I don't want the sensation my fingers experience on my exploration tour of his torso to end. But I have never kissed another guy. It is wrong. I shouldn't. I cannot.

Then again, I have also never fondled another guy's chest like this. Yet that feels okay just now.

Anyway, I stop him. The offender pulls away and radiates a bright and beautiful smile. He reaches for his washing towel and puts it over my eyes. I make an approach to take off the blindfold, but he places his finger on my lips, whispering "hushhhhhh!"

He guides my head to rest on the edge of the pool, tenderly pets my face and emulates a kiss with his fingers caressing my lips. His other hand fondles my chest and circles my nipples. With a deep sigh, I surrender myself to this treatment. My whole body shivers from anxiety and excitement.

While I wonder if it would be appropriate to explore this extraordinary chest some more, another hand begins to massage my member again carefully. It takes quite a while for my muddled mind to do the maths. When I realize it must be his mouth on my dick, I am already overwhelmed by the blissful things his tongue does, wrapped around the cherry. He lifts my body on top of the upper stair step with ease without interrupting his tongue duties. It feels so awesome. I just let it happen.

Just before he pushes me over the edge, he stops. I take off the blindfold, wondering what's going on. Blow boy sits up straight and smiles his brightest smile at my intimidated, expectant face. He starts petting my thighs with one hand and pulling on my scrotum with the other, making my whooping dick bobbing up and down while his fingers massage my balls.

On the last pull he pauses in the lowest position, still working the nuts. When he lets go, my dick swings up, splashes out of the water and snappily flaps on my abs. This set off my sperm gun. I blow multiple loads in pulsating blasts all over my torso.

"Hands free! Congrats! You are a quick learner", the sword master smirks after a few moments, leans in and gives me a brief yet intense kiss. Le Petit Mort has killed my resistance.

Then he turns around, walks across and steps out of the pool.

"Where are you going?" I whine after the inked spine mask.

Before he slides the door open, my accidental acquaintance turns around once more: "The geezer leaving here a few minutes ago has surely called the manager by now. They are extremely old-fashioned in this place regarding tattoos and stuff," he smiles, and while he vanishes, he adds "and remember: make sure you don't spoil the water if you don't want to get arrested."

I am left dazed and confused, my mind marveled, my body blotched and both completely drained, when just moments later, some noise behind the glass door sets off another adrenalin rush.

What will they do if, instead of Yakuza boy they are looking for, they find a foreigner with a hardon in their hot pool, covered in cum? Using the towel the fleeing assassin left behind I hastily rub the splooge off me. I move down to sit on the bottom of the pool, pulling my legs close to conceal my still erect cock.

My heart races as the door is pushed open.

Instead of the police squad I expect, yet another old man walks in.

It takes all the washing ceremony of this latest guest for my hypothalamus to clear the cache and my circulatory system to wash out the Oxytocin. Just as the old man enters the pool, I feel safe enough to snatch the tainted towel and rush out. I add to the list of my impeachable offenses not engaging in the mandatory washing ceremony before getting back to the lockers.

The hurry is imperative, though, because of my embarrassment, and also, because I hope to bump into my alluring acquaintance again. Not sure what to do or say if I did, but it feels like the most important thing this very moment.

FIRST CLASS FIRST TIME

Of course, he is gone.

Instead, I find a hand-written note with my things:

> "In a dark place
> we find ourselves
> and a little more knowledge
> lights our way.
> (Yoda)"

RICHARD T. GRAYSON

FIRST CLASS FIRST TIME

RED HEAT

Meet Dmitry

The odd melange of sky-high excitement and profound frustration Dan feels, as he arrives back at his hotel, can only be remediated by either a hard workout or an even harder party night out.

Dan's excitement stems from the recognition he got today from a top-grade investment firm, verifying the excellent potential of his software product and the soundness of his business plan. The potential investors had flown him into Moscow first-class yesterday, had invited him for dinner and drinks in an elite establishment last night and had treated had him like royalty ever since a driver in a classy uniform had picked him up at his arrival gate.

Dan had come to Moscow with high hopes to get the breakthrough he desperately needs. He is living off his savings and his parent's money for way too long already. A sizable cash injection in his start up was his last chance to make this thing fly. Hence, he was prepared to compromise on the terms of such investment.

The guys in the expensive suits liked his pitch. But they insisted on buying out the entire company. They had offered Dan to stay on the team as the chief software architect for a generous pay check. However, it would not be his baby anymore. The new owners could squeeze him out at their convenience.

Dan is not ready to accept such terms. He expects his software to revolutionize the industry and make many people rich; and he intends to be one of them. Even richer, much richer, than this buy-out offer would make him.

Thus, his frustration. Dan feels abused. If they had no intention to honor the conditions they had been discussing for weeks in the negotiations preceding this trip, why did they bring him here? Why get his hopes up?

He is not only excited that the professionals had validated his ideas. That he got them so greedy was proof to Dan that his concept was spot on. It is also the way he told the obtruders off. His performance in the big showdown quite enthused Dan, even though the meeting had ended in somewhat of a disaster. He had given the suits a fantastic speech, he thought, on his passion for the company, his determination to innovate, the ingenuity of his product and how he will now go it alone in this brutal world of fierce competition, and how he will eventually succeed against all odds. How this should work out? Dan had no clue. The suits probably knew that. Still, he felt great about himself after he had delivered that spontaneous monolog.

He may have used quite offensive language, though, when coming to the grand finale. He felt he needed to add a touch of groundedness to make the string of tacky clichés more credible; yet he isn't sorry for a single word. And all participants kept a civilized facade when they split ways.

In considering his options on his way back to the hotel which he had to do in a regular taxi, since the firm seemed to only offer chauffeur service as long as you played to their rules, Dan decided to go for two vodkas from the minibar plus a workout.

Thankfully, the fancy hotel his hosts had booked for him has a small gym, which is just what Dan needs after this rollercoaster day. Upon his return, though, his room key does not work and the snobby reception staff informs him that his reservation got canceled and that, unfortunately, the hotel is booked-out. It takes some financial incentive for the manager on duty to allow him back to his room for one more night at a ridicules rate. Dan's frustratometer graph explodes exponentially, even on a logarithmic scale, and in a graphical daydream he sees the front desk clerk as the Korean shop owner in 'Falling Down' and himself rampaging through the hotel lobby like Michael Douglas.
He downs the two vodkas in seconds.

On his way to the gym, Dan sends a WhatsApp to his fiancé to let her know he will call her in the morning. He is out of words for today, which is why he decided against going out and partying off all the mixed emotions.

The so called 'Wellness Center' is basic; more of an alibi to cater to the health-conscious segment. It's a rectangular space about the same size as his ridiculously large hotel room, with a multipurpose machine at one end and an extensive collection of dumbbells in a rack at the other. A running machine and a press bench with a weight stand complete the equipment; nothing fancy; but enough for a decent workout.

Dan appreciates that the place is abandoned at the late hour. Back home, he also works out the early or late hours because he hates the awkwardness of strangers sweating next to him. Dan never talks to anyone during workouts and in a confined place like this it would need more discipline to block out others than he could summon up tonight.

Dan starts his routine with a few sets of lightweight butterfly motions on the multipurpose machine. It is boiling in the compact room, and he develops a sweat right away; just what he came here for. He ups the weight for a final set and then goes for the press bench next.

Just as Dan starts his second set of bench presses, the gym door opens and a young man walks in. The rude intruder wears cut-off jeans shorts and an oversized t-shirt. Judging from this odd apparel, this misfit cannot be a regular to gyms, Dan reckons, nor does he fit in such an expensive business hotel. He looks familiar, but Dan can't figure out where he may have seen him before.

On top of being oddly displaced, the young guy appears disoriented and doesn't seem to even realize that someone else is present. That, however, is just fine with Dan; yet astonishing, considering how confined the space is. The dull look on this guy's face, Dan thinks, makes it well possible the douche needs his full concentration not to trip over his own feet. He might be one of the hotel's bellboys in those funny uniforms wearing those funny caps, and that's how I know him, Dan wonders, and that explains why he does not acknowledge him. He may have snuck in here violating house rules, not expecting guest working out this late.

Dan goes back to his routine. His new roommate starts his exercises with pull-ups. The bar is mounted to a wall behind the multipurpose machine, so Dan can hardly see the rookie. Yet ignoring him will not work because he can hear him. The ignorant intruder sighs loudly with every pull-up and moans even louder on the way down. He is churning out quite a few reps, though, and when Dan checks on him from the corner of his eye, the noise count stands at twenty-something already. Dan recognizes the alleged rookie is still going with decent form, chin above the bar on the top and extended arms all the way down. The jerk may not be new to lifting after all, he concedes. Instead of giving the guy at least some credit, though, Dan scorns again the inappropriateness of his outfit and goes back to his own exercise. He adds a few pounds to the dumbbells. For one, because it looks more impressive should his gym buddy realize him eventually, and second because the workout will now have to relief the extra aggression added to Dan's emotional state by having to actively ignore the coarse intruder.

After three acceleratingly noisy sets of pull-ups, the young penetrator walks across the entire gym, over to the wall of mirrors behind the dumbbell racks. He struts like a Wigger, Dan thinks to himself; like the beefy Russian Guidos with the thick necks and the tiny gold chains, thinking they are 'bad ass niggers', who Dan learned to hate ever since they started invading his favorite holiday spots.

This guy, though, doesn't look beefy at all in his oversized shirt. He reminds Dan of the Dobermann puppy his parents brought home when he was still a kid. On this puppy you could already see all the features that would soon develop into a muscle clung fighter dog, but it was still in a cute way.

There is nothing cute about the intruder puppy, though. He has a crude Slavic look to him with a peculiar, dull aggressiveness in the empty-headed face. Dan decides to call him Dmitry.

RICHARD T. GRAYSON

FIRST CLASS FIRST TIME

Even if Dan would consider socializing during workouts, Dmitry doesn't seem like an entertaining chatter at all. Everything about Dmitry's appearance puts Dan off, partly because he disturbed Dan's solitude; and simply because he absolutely wants to hate the planet tonight. The guy wears sizable brilliant studs in both earlobes and has slits cut in his groomed eyebrows. He sports a cutout stripe on the left side of his skull between the dramatic fades on the sides and much longer flashy red-colored hair on the top. He must be one of the bellboys with the funny cap hiding the silly haircut; otherwise Dan would certainly remember where he has seen this major jerk before.

Dmitry still overlooks Dan even as he walks past him, casually smiling at himself while approaching the mirrors, exposing a wide gap in very uneven teeth. When he smiles, he looks even more dull and appalling, Dan gripes.

Dmitry moves close to the mirrors, pulls up the sleeves of his shirt and flexes both arms. Dan is busy doing incline bench presses, struggling to manage the extra weight but cannot help glancing over to the posing puppy. As he gets a glimpse of Dmitry's sizable, Avocado-shaped bicep, he almost drops the barbell on his chest. He didn't quite expect that.

Dmitry also seems impressed by what the mirror shows him, flexes his jaw muscle and lifts an eyebrow. He contracts his biceps a few more times, eventually pulls the shirt over his head, drops it on the dumbbell rack and promptly reverts to more posing.

The youngster reveals a less inked and more toned body than Dan had expected to be hidden underneath the oversized garment. His smooth physique is decently athletic, yet not spectacular, even though it amazes Dan how much the biceps grow in sized when put to use, as Dmitry lifts his arms up again to show another pose.

The muscle puppy hurries his hands all over his upper body, briefly pausing on his abdominals while tensing every fiber in his torso. Dan insists on not being impressed.

To continue his workout, Dmitry goes for the quad curl machine. He moves shirtless across the room like huge bodybuilders do. The guys that have to walk around their way too massive thighs and who's way too massive latissimus muscles spread their arms outwards like John Wayne waiting for the shootout. This is how Dmitry walks. Only that his legs and lats are far from massive. You must be kidding me, Dan furrows his brow.

Halfway through the first set of quad curls, Dmitry seems to realize that tight cut-off jeans are not ideal for leg workouts. He collects his shirt from the dumbbell rack, folds it, then takes off the pants and stacks his gear neatly on the floor next to the quad machine.

Besides his high Lebrons, the only thing Dmitry now still wears is the tiniest piece of undergarment Dan has ever seen. This thong is barely big enough to cover his clean crotch. Delicate strings hold a tiny triangular piece of cloth in position. Dan considers commenting on this by laughing out loud but decides not to cause any attention, since he is glad the preposterous power pretender is all occupied with himself.

The skimpily clad jock does two more sets of leg raises before he walks over to the mirrors again to check on his progress.

He only briefly focuses on his legs though, possibly because they are not that remarkable, and goes back to posing his upper body.

Dan envisages how in ten years the youngster will

display the brutal features of the typical Russian bully with round shoulders and chubby muscularity. He already hits his poses with the confidence of a massive 220 pound iron addict, even though he may only weigh in at about 160 right now. Maybe that big guy is already what Dmitry sees in the mirror, Dan thinks, and he seems to appreciate his future self a lot more than Dan does.

Quite an antagonism to the hulking way the cocky teen hits his poses are the smooth twisting motions he makes transitioning from one pose to the next. Dmitry grooves and wiggles, shifting his bodyweight from one leg to the other. The cocky youngster erratically alternates between aggressive posing and prancing about.

This presentation appalls and fascinates Dan at the same time. He always found it cute to watch the newbies in his gym celebrate their first visible gains by mimicking the big guys in disarming earnestness. Yet this guy's pretentious show-off routine looks ridicules in the miniature thong. Still, Dan cannot help but watch out of the corner of his eye. He is trying hard to not show any obvious interest in the narcissistic display, and so far, Dmitry hasn't even glanced in Dan's direction once.

The way the rookie interacts with himself in the mirror reminds Dan of his Doberman again. The young dog used to bark at every reflection of himself in every mirror or shop window because he did not know it was him. He wanted to impress the other dog. In that same way it looks like the muscle puppy is starring down the guy in the mirror, trying to impress him by looking sexy or cool or flirtatious.

Dan cannot deny anymore certain elegance in the cocky poise of this young athlete. And yes, this guy's body is impressive, he has to admit. Yet the ridiculously tiny crotch cover and bragging big guy attitude still nauseate him.

Dmitry continues his routine with butterflys. Dan gets all hung up over the fact that the dripping flasher doesn't even bother to place a towel on the seat, even though his body is covered with nothing but sweat.

Dmitry churns out more repetitions with twice the weight Dan used earlier, moaning and groaning again on every move. The fly machine pumps up his pectoral muscles a little more on every repetition like balloons.

While Dan gradually develops some respect for the size the puppy's muscles have now grown to, the stupid grimaces Dmitry makes with every move put him off again. He advances his chin, which looks retarded, moans open-mouthed and produces all sorts of distorted facial expressions laboring the weights.

The moronic grimaces combined with almost obscene groaning sounds provoke porn movie flash backs in Dan's mind. His research in the vast collection of male muscle masturbation videos, he had secretly accumulated on the internet over the years, had yielded the off-turning realization that most of the leading men in such clips look appallingly stupid when pumping it. Just like Dmitry.

Dmitry does one set of flys after the other and in between the sets he walks up and down the gym, twisting and flexing his body, doing his dance moves and checking his progress. To displace the porn fantasies Dan recalls a poem he once read, of a panther who restlessly strolls up and down in his cage, eagerly awaiting a chance to put his enormous power to use.

The young athlete looks powerful indeed, Dan has to concede. From many angles the tiny strings of the thong are almost invisible, so he looks bare naked, with sweat covering his body like baby oil.

While the incoherent associations in his head still battle it out, Dan's phone buzzes. He cringes as if he fears this could draw the attention of the powerful predator. He hurries to the phone and switches it off, not without taking note that the incoming message was from his fiancé asking for the news of today. Dan doesn't want to be pulled back into the sobering realities of his normal life, now that he starts to develop particular fantasies about this more and more surreal encounter.

As he checks on Dmitry, the predator puppy still indulges in his narcissistic isolation. The exhausted athlete gasps for air open-mouthed as he performs haptic checks of his muscles on his way to the mirror wall. He sighs with every pose and approves his accomplishments by lifting an eyebrow, pursing his lips or squinting his eyes in turns. It genuinely looks like is coming on to the other dog in the mirror. He winks flirtatiously and his fingers even tenderly touch his lips a few times during the courtship performance. And then he puts on a tough-guy duck face for a change, lowering his head and looking at his counterpart with challenging aggression.

Dan detects a growing bulge less and less concealed by the tiny lycra. More than once the philandering poser reaches into the stretched fabric, a little too long to just be adjusting an itching pecker. It looks like Dmitry is turning himself on.

That, weirdly, turns Dan on. What was appalling, only a few minutes ago, now seems rather alluring. A captivating composition of cocky arrogance and playful fun on young Dmitry when wooing himself, the grooving motions, the awkward facial expressions, even the tiny garment trigger an arousal he cannot dismiss anymore. While he is meticulously avoiding displaying any kind of concern for the performance, he also has to work hard not to get hard. Or better yet: work out hard; because the approach he comes up with is to churn out ever more reps. Soon, though, he worries, he will not be able to hide his interest.

He is just glad that Dmitry's sole concern still seems to be himself. Occasionally, though, it almost looks like the young show-boater is well aware how awkward this self-indulged attempt to seduce his own mirror image is. In these moments an astounded wide-eyed glance and an ironic smile whoosh across his face and Dan fears the young narcissist could awake out of his self-centeredness.

Dmitry now picks up a pair of heavy dumbbells and

starts a set of alternating curls. Again, he moans on every curl and even more sweat pours from his inflated, bare chest. After an impressive number of repetitions, he drops the weights and puffs up his glistening, swollen body in a triumphant double biceps pose one more time.

Dan stares breathlessly at the staggeringly sculpted specimen, mesmerized by the young man's presumptuousness and overbearing confidence. He hastily picks up the barbell again and starts what must be his 15th set of bench presses.

From the corner of his eyes, he notices that Dmitry has now picked much lighter weights, and this time is facing his bench.

While Dmitry pumps more and more blood in the thick veins running along the peaks of his massive arms, the same happens in Dan's crotch. The excitement will show in his sweat pants any moment now. To hide it at least a bit, he puts the barbell back into the stand and sits up straight. Dan's knees shake at the thought of tenting in front of the sweat covered, nearly naked athlete, but he can't figure out an exit strategy.

Dmitry has moved closer and closer towards the bench. Dan is so occupied exorcizing his inner demons bombarding his mind with flashbacks of his favorite muscle worship videos that he only now realizes the youngster's bulge has almost grown to full size. Just like his own. With every curl, with every step Dmitry's pecker obscenely stretches the lycra even more. A second later it snakes out of the string with verve.

Dmitry comes to a halt one step away from the bench, gasping for air, pouring with sweat and with his sizable, now uncovered boner pointing straight at Dan's face. Dan is frozen like a rabbit in sight of that snake.

"You help me" Dmitry utters with a heavy Russian accent. Dan is not sure if Dmitry is referring to the weights or his snake. There is nothing he could do about the weights. So he wonders what he is supposed to do with the sizable serpent.

The sweat covered muscle guy takes two more steps

towards the bench. The tip of his pecker is now just inches away from Dan's mouth.

"Pull down pant!" Dmitry commands. Dan doesn't move, scared shitless of what might unfold next, yet too excited and too curious to just get up and leave or tell the muscle stud off.

"Ok! You shy," concedes Dmitry and lets go of the weights. The dumbbells hit the carpet floor with a loud clank.
He pulls down the thong, reaches for Dan's hands and places them on his sweaty chest.
"You want to touch me whole time, or not?" ask Dmitry with a commanding voice.
Did he detect his staring after all, Dan wonders, desperately trying to think straight? He would love to explore the young guy's amazing torso yet does not dare to move his hands. Neither does he want to pull away.

Dmitry grabs Dan's wrists. He rhythmically flexes and relaxes his muscles as he direct Dan's fingers to explore the massive mountain range. Then he makes Dan's palm shovel the inflated lump upwards against gravity. Next, he slides it towards the abdominal valley, giving him the opportunity to touch every gorge and every hill sculptured of rock-hard muscle.

"Now you help me." He wraps Dan's fingers around his most pumped up part and slides them back and forth a few times. When he lets go, Dan tightens the grip and continues choking the young Russian's stiffened sidewinder while still hastily fondling his tensed torso. The rabbit's intimidation is repressed by the muscle addict's inquisitiveness as he fears the opportunity may not last very long.

Dmitry advances his pelvis, pushes his boner right in Dan's face and reaches for his head.

"Take it in your mouth, that big dick" he commands and shoves his prick into Dan's throat.

With no practical experience in giving or even receiving a blow job, Dan timidly starts sucking on the mushroom head the way he has seen it in many of the juicier videos he secretly enjoys. While he licks away on the muscle stud's pecker, he fumbles with his ball sack as he would want it done to himself, but never dared to suggest to any of his girlfriends.

"Take off shirt! Let's add challenge", Dmitry instructs, pulling back and reaching for Dan's sweat pants, exposing his hardon saluting his dominator with quite a bit of pre-cum on the top. Dmitry picks up the dumbbells while Dan rips off his shirt as he was instructed.

The young athlete raises the weights right above Dan's head, holding them steady. Leaning back and balancing the heavy load, the fiber bundles in the athlete's ripped torso are strung to breaking point.

Dan is hypnotized by Dmitry's swirl shaped belly button threatening to pop out. He goes back to exploring the ripped physique, while the young man moans ever louder from the struggle of holding the weights firmly above Dan's head.

"Quick. My dick!" accidentally rhymes the young man.

Dan does as he is told and rushes back to his head job duties. If the guy drops the iron now, it will hit him right on the head like a fifty-pound hammer, he thinks. This seems to be a competition for what the Russian athlete can hold for longer: the weights or the outburst. This makes sense to Dan just now; in a twisted way. Dmitry's gasping gets faster and so does Dan's stroking. The young jock's body shivers from the strain of the stamina race of virility.

"Quick" he shouts again, moaning and groaning. The exhausted racer bends his back ever further, starts convulsing, but still holds up the dumbbell with shaking arms. Dan maximizes jerking speed, determined to win this race.

"I'm going to come!" howls Dmitry and spreads his shaking arms to a crucifix. Dan beats the muscle guy's stick in hard and hasty final strokes. He leans back, preparing for what is about to cum. Two beats later, Dmitry explodes. The massive ejaculation sends spasms through his shaking body, causing him to let go of the dumbbells. The clank of iron hitting the floor accentuates loads two and three of six shots of cum raining all over Dan.

"Good job!" Dmitry puffs and blows while his pec muscles jump up and down.

The wheezing flexer smiles down at his erect prick in relief. Both men enjoy the accomplishment for a few quiet seconds, drowned out by both guy's heavy breathing.

Then the muscle stud leans forward and nuzzles Dan down to the backrest. Dan grabs the opportunity and the rounded pecs that had jumped to full contraction.

Dmitry slowly advances ever closer. He kisses Dan, who can't figure out if he wants to resist, immersed in this overwhelming experience and confused by the new and exciting emotions, so much that he does not even pay attention to the sudden sensation of something touching his dick. Until he realizes that Dmitry now sits on his cock and humps up and down in his lap while continuing to kiss him ever more intensely.

Panic overcomes Dan. He does not want this. He has

never plugged a guy, nor has he even ever considered doing so, not even when masturbating while watching man

on man porn. And yet, he doesn't want this to stop. Just a few minutes ago Dan had projected all his anger and aggression, hatred and paranoia, his disdain and contempt of the world onto this detestable narcissist. The world that had screwed him so badly. Now he gets to fuck this narcissist; and in that, he fucks the world back for being so appalling, yet alluring. Again, twistedly, this makes sense to Dan just now.

Dmitry stops the kiss. He sits up straight and starts twisting, turning and circling his pelvis in Dan's lap, creating a multitude of so far unknown sensations. Dan's limbic system experiences significant latency from sensation to perception, because at the same time his visual unit uploads feeds of a glistening muscle torso dancing in his lap. Dan's brain and body threaten to blue-screen due to emotional and physical overload. Just before he would go into forced hibernation, he pumps his upload inside Dmitry.

"Wow. All the way in my mouth" smiles Dmitry and releases a big wad of white fluid from his pursed lips right on target on his still hard cock. It takes Dan's hibernated processor an eternity to compute that the young athlete is just messing with him.

"My turn!", Dmitry cheers, jumps up, reaches for Dan's legs, rolls him up and forces his cock up Dan's ass. With some delay, the visuals and with even more delay the sensations arrive at his brain, but Dan is incapable of initiating any reaction. Even when the stabbing pain from penetrating his tight virgin ass hits him, he only utters a hushed "Ddddon't!". For a brief second Dan fears he might get unconscious.

When Dmitry was riding Dan's cock, he moved as smoothly and elegantly as he did when he was prancing through the gym during his workout. The top in him, however, is as tough-guy as his bodybuilder poses were, no frills, no twists, no turns, just exhibiting power. In the rhythm of the aggressive thrusts of his pelvis, his chest muscles bounce up and down. In his agony, Dan doesn't even know whether he presses his hands against the pounding pecs to push back the penetrator or to perceive his power. As the pain eases, though, a fresh stream of amazing sensations swiftly overwhelms his anxieties.

"Let's add challenge again!" Dmitry commands, squinting at the barbell above Dan's head: "push weight!"

Dan follows the order, both men grab the bar and Dan starts pushing.

The dominator syncs up his thrusts with Dan's exercise, ramming his dick up Dan's anus with every push of the weight. And just as Dan cannot do another rep and drops the barbell back in the stand, Dmitry releases his big shot with the snarl of a panther. With the aggressive penetrator's final thrust, also Dan's dick squeezes out two more globs.

Dmitry retreats, smiles to himself in satisfaction, gets up, walks over to collect his gear, dresses back up and walks out the door without one more word or glance over to Dan.

The events that just occurred puzzle Dan in so many ways, his mind just went blank. Lost in reverie, he stares at the door for quite a while. He leans back and closes his eyes.

When he hears the door opening again, he looks up expecting Dmitry to come back. Yet an elegant gray-haired gentleman in a three-piece suit heads straight towards him.

The gentleman pulls a chair from the wall next to the bench and sits down.
"Good evening, Sir. May I introduce myself to you? My name is Winston Wadsworth. I work for Linklater & Partners in London."
Dan, still in buffer overflow mode, looks at the stranger with an empty expression on his face.

"First, let me express my disaffirmation for the somewhat brutish way you were eventually coerced by our young friend into sexual conduct you, at least initially, seemed to disapprove of."

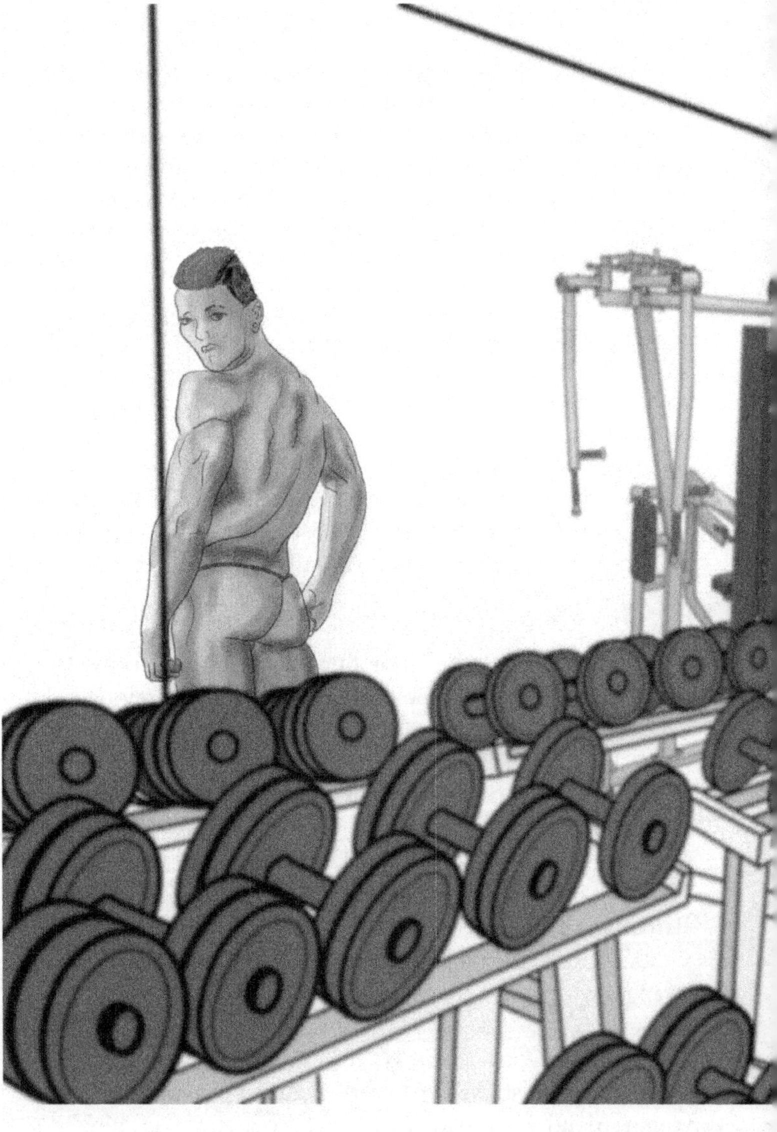

FIRST CLASS FIRST TIME

'What?' Dan's facial expression asks, though his lips open without uttering a sound. He isn't sure whether this sentence would have made any sense to him, even in full possession of his mental capabilities.

"How do you...?"

"Well, it was rather obvious, I thought, you initially disapproved of the anal penetration you were subjugated to. You seemed to enjoy the other variations of your encounter, though. Not to mention the two climaxes," the older gentlemen ignores Dan's actual question.

"I mean, how do you know what just happened?", Dan insists, gradually regaining his composure.

The arrogant attorney continues to evade Dan's question: "Oh. Apologies again. I should have started from the beginning. I represent the company you met with today and I am here to extend an offer to you on their behalf."

"This is not a good time" Dan jadedly utters, leaning back and closing his eyes.

"Well, I'm afraid it is the only appropriate time, Sir, to explain to you the special conditions of our offer."

When opening his eyes again, Dan realizes that he is naked and covered with cum. He reaches for his sweat pants, puts them on and looks for his shirt.
"Can we not discuss this tomorrow?", he says while he puts his shirt back on.

"Well, tomorrow will be too late, I'm afraid. The urgency is determined by the events that just transpired. I'm afraid we will have to come to an agreement tonight,

Sir."

"Agreement on what? And what does 'too late' mean?" asks Dan, intending to come back to his original question later.

The attorney readjusts his posture: "I should inform you that the young gentlemen you just engaged with will be considered a minor in the court of law, in case we bring tonight's incident to the attention of the authorities. Sexual activities with a minor are not dealt with lightly in this country."

"No way is this guy under age. He definitely looks grown up to me," Dan shouts.

"Well, looks can be deceiving, can't they? Certain parts of this young gentleman were quite grown up during the act, I will concede to you, Sir," the gray suit chuckles.
"With regard to the legal repercussions: what you know or believe is of no importance, I'm afraid, Sir."

"This was none of my fault. The sucker seduced me big time."

"Well, it can be debated who the sucker was in this encounter, can't it, Sir?" the cunning counselor concludes.

"Anyway: why should I believe you? Show me proof he is under age!"

"I did not say he *is* underage, Sir. I explicitly said, he will be considered as such."

Dan looks puzzled.

"It is pretty simple: Your young friend originates from

a tiny village far to the east of this wide country. In these parts of the Russian Federation, local administration is not very advanced. In other words: public registers are rudimentary, to say the least. Honestly, out there, for the appropriate amount of money in an envelope handed to the right people, you can get the papers to prove whatever you want to prove. You should rather not build your strategy on the ability to contest that we can produce evidence for your misconduct and the inappropriate age of your friend."

"This damn hustler is not my friend. I did not even know him until an hour ago."

"Well, it is up to you, Sir, to determine what you call people that you have sexual relationships with. This is none of my concern…."
"I do not have a relationship with this sucker, damn it!" Dan snaps.
"Well, Sir, it is off course as well entirely up to you to determine which relationship status you consider an appropriate basis to engage in intercourse…"

"And as I said, Sir: It's of no importance. What is important, though, is, besides the fact that your friend is rather young, you were additionally engaging in unnatural sexual conduct. The gay rights movement is not all that popular with the authorities here in Russia, as I am sure you are aware."

"I'm not gay. I am happily married", Dan shouts, exaggerating the status of his relationship with his fiancé to make his point.

"Well Sir, I believe you will not want to contest that you just had oral and anal intercourse with another male."

FIRST CLASS FIRST TIME

"Active and passive, I might add, or top and bottom, as I believe they call this in notorious circles. In the usual definition, and, more importantly, in Russian legislation, these are considered homosexual acts. One may think you would not want to tell your fiancé about this particular episode of your trip, would you, Sir?"

"I could well dispute any such allegations. You cannot prove a thing. My wife will never believe you."

"You are being naïve, Sir, if you don't mind me being so frank. Your fiancé is of no concern to us, however. I suggest she should not be your concern either, just now. And, I may add a personal advice: given the preferences we are talking about here, not in the future either." The corny counselor smirks, delighted with his lecture.

"There are far more severe consequences than relationship trouble to be dealt with here," the gray geezer continues.

"Let me start of by explaining how the young gentlemen came to works for us. We have picked the young men to best suit your preferences, which we have determined from analyzing your profile history on numerous gay websites that you frequently visit. The time you spend on these kinds of websites surprised us, I must add."

"..."

"Obviously, our AI has matched your tastes pretty well. I must say, the young man has a remarkable similarity to the leading man in one or two of your most often re-played pornographic videos. You seem to have a distinct preference for the more... how shall I put it... more proletarian type. And for athletic physiques off course."

"..."

"By the way, you can feel save: we have assured ourselves of the impeccable health status of this youngster. We do not want to risk any medical consequences from this encounter."

"You hacked my profiles? This is illegal! I could sue you!"

The evil advocate looks down on Dan and just lifts an eyebrow.

"Anyway: the guy practically raped me. I can testify on that. It's his word against mine."

"You may not have comprehended it yet, but this entire hotel and off course this gymnasium, are equipped with high resolution close circuit cameras. We have a video of this last hour that could just as well be featured on one of your preferred websites, if you allow me this remark. It might sell extremely well, I could imagine," the suited guy chuckles in awkward high voice sounds.

"Thinking about it: that's another option…", he sinisterly insinuates.

"… and, in case this did not yet convince you of the overwhelming body of evidence…" the smartass solicitor pauses and chuckles again in his high voice about his own choice of words, "medical examination, if need be, will find your ejaculated semen in the young gentleman's anus."

Panic creeps up on Dan. And rage.

"What the fuck do you want?" he shouts.

The brutal barrister chuckles, this time for Dan's choice of word.

"There is no reason for uncivilized behavior. Nothing bad has to result from any of this."

"How is that?"

"First, let me please continue my explanation of the terrible things that could happen. That we are on the same page as to the benefits of the deal I will suggest to you in due cause."

"Let us assume for a moment that we do report tonight's incident to the authorities, which we have no intention to do, I want to emphasize, in the case you show a cooperative attitude. This would lead to your immediate arrest. The authorities would not allow you to leave the country tomorrow. Instead, you would be confined in a detention facility and would have to await trial there. I would suggest sparing us any details on the conditions in Russian detention facilities, and the treatment to be expected there; especially with child molesters and homosexuals; and in your case: both."

"But you said, nothing bad has to come from this," Dan wails.

"And it doesn't. The company I represent is prepared to make you a generous offer. All you have to do is accept this offer and tonight's incident could be a faint and hopefully pleasant memory soon."

"What kind of offer?"

"The company I represent provided you with a proposal today to take over one hundred percent of your business, didn't they?"

"You had chosen to decline this offer, presumptuously. While using quite uncivilized language, I was told."

FIRST CLASS FIRST TIME

"…"

"This offer still stands, subject to you signing the contractual arrangements tonight. I am afraid we cannot allow you to leave the country prior to us settling this matter. Nor this hotel, I may add. I'm sure you understand."

"You're crazy!"

"No need to become personal, Sir. I am just the messenger, mind you. My client believes this is a very generous offer, given your… let's call it unfavorable negotiating position right now."
"You are free to take a shower and thoroughly consider our proposal. I will come to your room in one hour with the paperwork. Room 407, isn't it?"

"A piece of advice as a sign of good will: if you do not want a shower scene added to your first personal porn video you may want to consider placing a towel over the useless valve in the top corner of your shower cabin," the devilish advocate whispers conspiratorially.

The suited executioner gets up, turns to the door and back to Dan again: "One more thing: we uploaded the video of your… workout… to your Dropbox account. Your special one, which you do not share with your fiancé, I should point out. The one you use to store your juicy collection," the geezer smiles. "In case you want to verify the quality of the close-ups and money shots…," he chuckles with an even higher pitch as he walks out.

In the door frame, he turns around once more: "Oh. Do you want me to bring along our young friend when I come to your room later? The number of climaxes tonight will not make any difference, regardless of your decision for glory or Gulag. You may just as well get the most out of this… engagement," he chuckles. "In the best case, you can consider it a welcome boner… ahem… bonus."

Dan grabs a weight plate and troughs it after the gray suit, only hitting the slamming door.
He drops from the bench and crumps into an embryonic position. The excitement, the rage, the panic, all dissolve into a state of complete despair. Dan bursts out into tears.

ACKNOWLEDGMENTS

The setting in 'Red Heat' was inspired by some steaming hot videos on Fitcasting.com.

The character and features of the young Asian in 'Cherry Blossom' were inspired by the amazing photography of Asian male physiques by the artists at Altaclub and Seangraphy.

The background in the drawing on page 92/93 is based on a photo by ©Scott Norris Photography licensed via Shutterstock. The background in the drawing on page 96/97 is based on a photo by ©on_france licensed via Shutterstock.

For the artwork in this book I used the fantastic tool Krita by KDE.

Many thanks for all the inspiration.

Made in the USA
Columbia, SC
08 January 2021